Scribbles

written and illustrated by
Theresa Mackiewicz

Scribbles stared at the math on the blackboard with her big brown eyes, and she began to frown. It was the beginning of the school year, and Scribbles was having problems learning this math already. She would rather be drawing, so her friends named her Scribbles even though her real name was Theresa. Scribbles drew when she was in math and English class. It didn't matter what subject she was in, as she always wanted to draw. Her pictures were simply amazing. She was truly an artist.

Whenever Scribbles went to school, she always got distracted. She wanted to draw all the time. Her teachers got mad at Scribbles because she never passed any of her schoolwork.

Day after day Scribbles drew pictures in class. Day after day she got in trouble with her teachers, especially with Mr. Stanza, her math teacher.

Mr. Stanza would always say to Scribbles in a harsh voice, "Theresa, if you don't stop drawing right now, you will fail this class! Not only will you fail this class, but you will be going to the principal's office for good!"

But one day, there was something different.

Scribbles went into class with her green froggy shirt, her favorite froggy hair ribbons, and her froggy jewelry. She sat down and got ready for math class. When she looked around, she saw another teacher in the classroom. She introduced herself as Mrs. Sunshine. Scribbles thought, *Hmmm....now I have two teachers. I wonder why?* But that thought passed, and she just watched Mrs. Sunshine.

Scribbles thought to herself, *This teacher is going around to all the students. She is helping everyone.*

Scribbles kept watching Mrs. Sunshine.

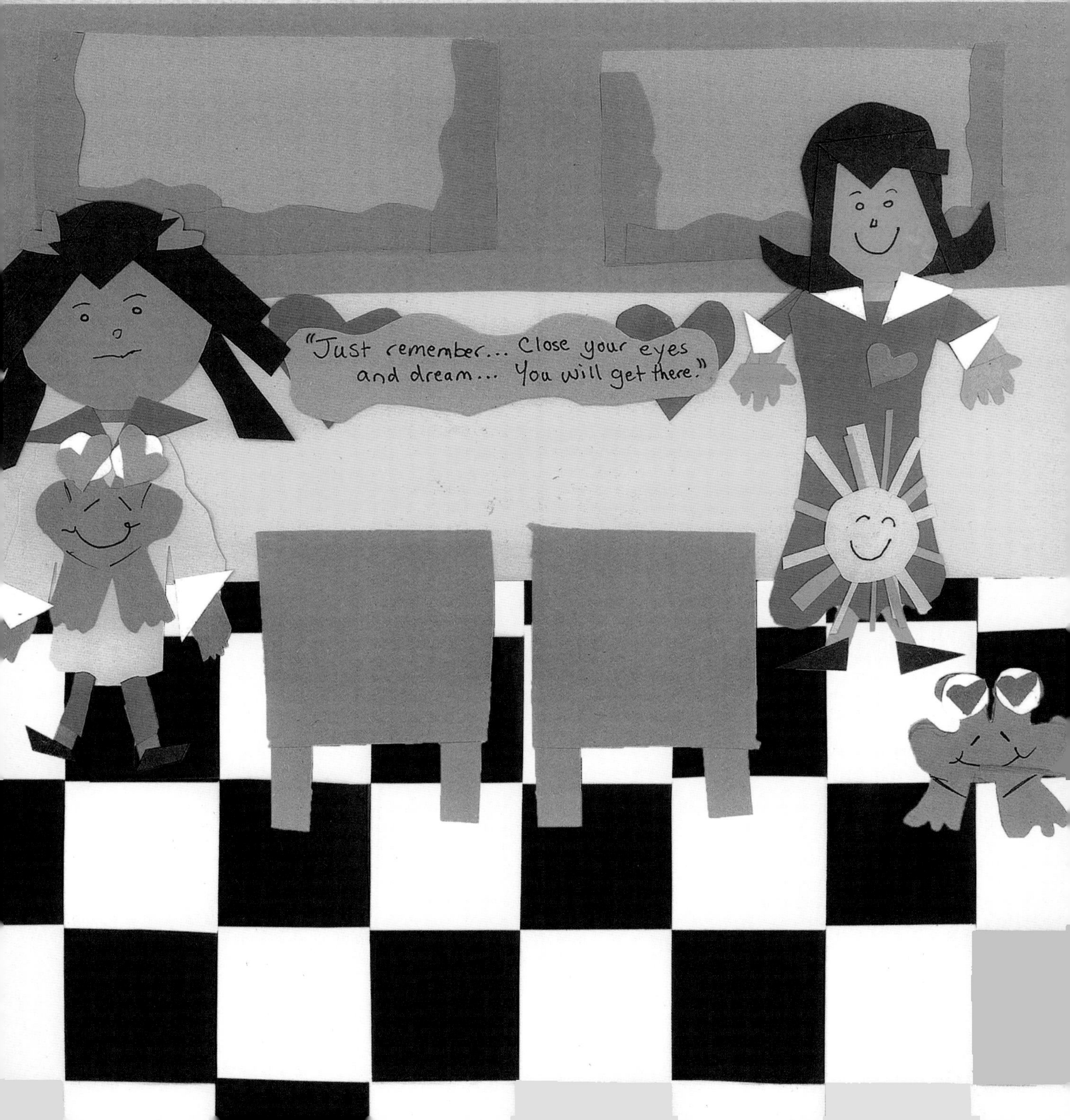
"Just remember... Close your eyes and dream... You will get there."

Mrs. Sunshine was intrigued by Scribbles' drawings.

"Well…you are a mighty fine artist. What else can you draw? Boy, someone really likes frogs," Mrs. Sunshine said with a smile and walked away.

Mrs. Sunshine wanted to know why Scribbles didn't do any of her assignments. She also wondered why she was failing her math and English classes. So, Mrs. Sunshine went over to Scribbles and asked her about frogs.

"Theresa, do you like frogs?" Mrs. Sunshine asked.

Scribbles was surprised that she was not in trouble with the teacher for drawing. Of course Scribbles was drawing frogs again.

Scribbles said, "Yes, I love froggies," in a sweet, soft voice.

Mrs. Sunshine smiled and whispered, "I have something for you."

Scribbles was surprised and asked, "What? Why?"

Mrs. Sunshine picked out of her pocket a sticker of a girl frog named Fancy.

Scribbles asked, "Why did you give this to me? I really do not deserve this sticker." She frowned and looked down.

Mrs. Sunshine asked, "Why don't you think you deserve it? I am sure you try really hard in all your classes."

Scribbles looked down still frowning. "I am failing in all my classes, even this one."

Scribbles took out her colored pencils. Mrs. Sunshine already knew this information, but she wanted Scribbles to tell her.

Then Scribbles started to draw again. Scribbles was looking for her favorite color, green of course, in her colored pencil pack.

Scribbles then looked up at Mrs. Sunshine as she held up her green colored pencil and said, "Green like froggies."

Mrs. Sunshine said with a smile on her face, "You really like to draw, and you are very good at it."

Scribbles said, "No, I am not. People always say that, but they don't really mean it."

Mrs. Sunshine said, "No really, you can draw! You put so much effort into it."

Scribbles looked up at her from the desk with sad eyes and said, "Really? No one ever told me that I was really good at drawing. Sometimes math is too hard, so I sit here and draw to take away the pain of not understanding like the rest of the kids in class. They always seem to understand math, where I can't figure it out, so I sit and draw. Usually my teachers, especially Mr. Stanza, take my artwork and throw it away. He usually says that my drawings are simply trash! My froggies are my happiness and Mr. Stanza just throws them away. I guess I understand, because math comes easy to him, but for me math is way too difficult."

Mrs. Sunshine, a special teacher who makes learning easier, told Scribbles she was a great artist, but to get good grades she needed to do some class work too. Mrs. Sunshine felt if Scribbles could feel confident, then she would succeed.

Scribbles looked at her with her big, beautiful, brown eyes and said, "Okay I'll try, but it is hard for me. I need that help you do during class. You know when you go around to everyone and ask if they understand the math? I also like when you ask Mr. Stanza questions about math so I don't feel stupid. It is like you read my mind. You know exactly what I am thinking."

Mrs. Sunshine said, "I can help you. Do you think your teacher goes too fast sometimes? I can slow him down for you."

Scribbles said, "Really?" with a surprised look. "But, but, can I draw too?"

Mrs. Sunshine responded, "Of course you can still draw. You certainly do not want to lose that talent of yours! But, you only can draw when we do not need to get schoolwork done, okay? Sometimes you can draw out a math problem and see it in a different way. Every student thinks differently. Just remember…close your eyes and dream… you will get there."

The next day, Scribbles came into school with a big smile on her face! She was so happy! Mrs. Sunshine greeted her with just as big of a smile and a warm welcome.

Mrs. Sunshine asked, "Are you ready to work and draw?"

Scribbles responded, "Yes, but are you ready to help me?"

Mrs. Sunshine laughed and said with a smile, "Of course I will help you! As long as you remember to close your eyes and dream…we will get there together."

Not only was Mrs. Sunshine in Scribbles' math class, but now she was in her English class too. English was Scribbles' first class of the day. Scribbles had to write a paragraph and draw a picture to go with it. This assignment was right up Scribbles' alley.

"What a great project," said Mrs. Sunshine with a smirk. She was wearing a green frog pin on her shirt. "Scribbles, this is a perfect assignment for you!"

Scribbles looked up at the sound of Mrs. Sunshine's voice and then noticed the green frog on her shirt.

"Did you wear that for me, Mrs. Sunshine?" Scribbles asked with a smile from ear to ear.

Mrs. Sunshine responded with a smile and a wink back at Scribbles, "I did especially for you. Let's see what you got kid. Knock 'em dead."

Scribbles knew she could do this assignment! Scribbles jumped right into her classwork. She worked really hard. She wrote about her favorite subject, frogs. After she was done with the writing, she started drawing her frog picture immediately.

"Boy, Theresa, you are working very hard! I am very proud and impressed with your focus and writing," Mrs. Sunshine stated with a smile.

Theresa looked up and smiled, "I am going to get an A on this assignment!"

Little did Scribbles know that Mrs. Sunshine made up the assignment for the English teacher, Ms. Lafonda. Mrs. Sunshine knew that in order for Scribbles to feel successful, she needed a really creative assignment. Mrs. Sunshine changed Ms. Lafonda's lesson plan to help Scribbles out. Mrs. Sunshine knew if she could engage Scribbles in a writing and drawing assignment, her self-esteem would rise. Putting a drawing with writing would be a perfect assignment for Scribbles. Mrs. Sunshine had done this assignment before to motivate students like Scribbles.

Scribbles drew and drew. She looked up and thought, *I cannot wait to show Ms. Lafonda and Mrs. Sunshine this.* Ms. Lafonda believed in Scribbles. She just wanted Scribbles to work hard and do well in school. Scribbles held her assignment up high and smiled from ear to ear.

Scribbles said, "Look, Mrs. Sunshine, I am done! Can I show Ms. Lafonda now?"

Mrs. Sunshine said, "Theresa, you did a nice job! How do you feel?"

"I feel great!" said Scribbles.

Scribbles took her paper to Ms. Lafonda shaking with fear. "Here Ms. Lafonda," Scribbles said in a trembling voice.

"Oh...I am so proud of you, Theresa!" Ms. Lafonda said with a great big smile.

Ms. Lafonda asked, "Theresa, can I show the other students your work? You did such a great job! Look at this picture. The frog is so wonderful! How did you draw this? Better yet, can I put it on my bulletin board because this deserves an A++!"

Scribbles was so excited that Ms. Lafonda loved her artwork and paragraph. She jumped up and down and let out an enthusiastic, "Of course!"

Ms. Lafonda said, "WOW! I knew you could do it! I love the picture, and I can't wait to read your work. You ROCK! Thank you very much."

Scribbles ran back to Mrs. Sunshine, and told her the whole story. She gave Mrs. Sunshine a great big hug and said, "Thank you! But I still need you in math. Can you help me?"

Mrs. Sunshine said, "Of course!"

Mrs. Sunshine read over Scribbles' file and understood that Scribbles did need some help in math. Scribbles needed to learn using a step-by-step process. Mrs. Sunshine realized that Mr. Stanza needed to start teaching slowly and when he put the problem on the board, he needed to label each step. Scribbles just needed to be taught in a different way in math, but with Mrs. Sunshine and Mr. Stanza's help, Scribbles just needed to close her eyes and dream…she would get there.

Mrs. Sunshine said, "Now you can do anything you put your mind to!"

When Mrs. Sunshine explained to Mr. Stanza how to teach Scribbles, he was able to help Scribbles feel successful. When Mrs. Sunshine and Mr. Stanza worked together, they made math come alive for all children, especially for Scribbles.

Scribbles made the honor roll for the rest of the year!

Acknowledgments

Benedict Mackiewicz III, my loving husband who always supports me, especially in my writing career.

Jerry Goldstein, who I give special thanks for being *Scribbles'* editor and my long time, good friend who has pushed me to reach my personal goals.

Y3K Tutor In Your Home: www.Y3KTutorInYourHome.com

My twin sons, Benedict Mackiewicz IV and Alexander Mackiewicz, who helped me with my artwork and suggestions.

Jeanette De Guzman, who read all of my work in the rough draft phase and positively motivated me.

Mila Goldshteyn, a dear friend who motivated me to keep writing and always supported me through the publishing process.

Becky Brennecke, who read my work at the final stage and helped me explore publishers.

Monica Henderson-Carpenter, who supported me in my writing.

To my family, especially Mom and Dad, and close friends, for always believing in me. Thank you for always being in my life and for your support. I love you forever.

To: All my former students.
I am very proud of you!

WAIT THERE'S MORE!

The learning and fun with *Scribbles* is just beginning. Now it is your child's turn to learn from Mrs. Sunshine! Be sure to go to **www.tmackbooks.com** and find the *Scribbles Companion Manual*. A total of thirty-two pages of everything you need to be Mrs. Sunshine yourself and make a difference in a young learner's life. Each PDF file contains strategies that Mrs. Sunshine uses.

Each PDF file is a step-by-step how-to manual explaining each educational strategy mentioned in *Scribbles* in great depth. Also the *Scribbles Companion Manual* demonstrates each of the activities so simply with full color pictures that a novice parent to an experienced educator could replicate each in a flash. Let YOUR student enjoy Mrs. Sunshine's lessons in the comfort of your own home or classroom. There is so much more to do and so much more to learn!

Scribbles Strategies and Activities List

Writing and Math Strategies
Strategies List: Writing
1. In a small group, re-teach the struggling students to build confidence.
2. Can-of-Worms *(See Scribbles Companion Manual at www.tmackbooks.com)*
3. Cloud→ to simple words→ to paragraphs *(See Scribbles Companion Manual at www.tmackbooks.com)*

Strategies List: Math
1. Step-by-step break down of the problem.
2. Drawing the math problem on the side of the page. *(See Scribbles Companion Manual at www. tmackbooks.com)*
3. Put problems in picture form. *(See Scribbles Companion Manual at www.tmackbooks.com)*

Writing and Math Activities:
Writing:
1. Make a Fancy the Frog to read to. Students can create a frog of their own or read to their pet at home. **(See *Scribbles Companion Manual* at www.tmackbooks.com for frogs to cut out)**
2. Make up a problem and try to stump the other student. **(See Mrs. Sunshine's Game in *Scribbles Companion Manual* at www.tmackbooks.com)**

Math:
1. Put problems in picture form.
2. Make up a problem and try to stump the other student. **(See Mrs. Sunshine's Game in *Scribbles Companion Manual* at www.tmackbooks.com)**

To follow Mrs. Sunshine visit:

 www.tmackbooks.com  facebook.com/tmackbooks  @tmackbook